GREAT
DAY
for

UP

By Dr. Seuss

Pictures by Quentin Blake

HarperCollins *Children's Books*

A CIP record for this title is available from the British Library.
No part of this publication may be reproduced, stored in a
retrieval system or transmitted in any form or by any means,
electronic, mechanical, photocopying, recording or otherwise,
without the prior permission of HarperCollins Publishers Ltd,
77-85 Fulham Palace Road, Hammersmith, London W6 8JB.

1 3 5 7 9 10 8 6 4 2
ISBN: 978-0-00-732454-5

Great Day For Up

Published by arrangement with Random House Inc., New
York, USA
First published in the UK in 1975
This edition published in the UK in 2009 by HarperCollins
Children's Books, a division of HarperCollins Publishers Ltd,
77-85 Fulham Palace Road, London W6 8JB

The HarperCollins website address is www.harpercollins.co.uk

Printed and bound in Hong Kong

UP!
UP!

The sun is getting up.

The sun gets up.

So UP with you!

UP!

Ear number one . . .

Ear number two.

Up, heads!

Up, whiskers!

Tails!

UP! UP!

Great day, today!
Great day
for

UP!

Up! Up!

You!
Open up
your eyes!

You worms!

You frogs!

You butterflies!

Up, whales!

Up, snails!

Up, rooster!

Hen!

Up!

Girls and women!

Boys and men!

Great day
for UP FEET!
Lefts and rights.

And **Up! Up!** Baseballs! Footballs! Kites!

Great day
to sing
up on a wire.

UP!

Up, voices!
Louder! Higher!

Up stairs!

Up ladders!

Up on stilts!

Great
day
for up
Mt. Dill-ma-dilts.

Everybody's doing **UP**s*!*

On bikes . . .

. . . and trees

. . . and buttercups.

UP! UP!

Waiters!

Alligators!

UP!

Up giraffes!

Great day
for seals!

Great day for UP
on ferris wheels!

UP! UP! UP!

Fill up the air.

Up, flags!
Balloons!
UP! Everywhere!

UP! UP! UP!

Great day for UP!

Wake every person,
pig and pup,
till EVERYONE
on Earth is up!

Except for me.
Please go away.
No **up.**
I'm sleeping in today.